VALEDICTION

Sitting in my bath for an hour in the darkness before dawn, steam mingling with the breeze from the open window. I savour the sounds of the distant city coming slowly to life and picture all those I know out there waking or turning over, taking the first bitter swig of the day's coffee. Laughing or weeping, some others cold and at peace forever beneath the mothering curve of the vast and splendid earth. And I wonder what it meant: all these monkey bodies and hands and kisses reaching out for each other, the sweet warmth of all our individual little packages of aloneness straining desperately against each other, so vulnerable and afraid. We were each in our own way poignant and pathetic, things our mothers would never knowingly have let loose, never trusted to be out there on our own in the world. But here we are each trying to do good but so often doing harm, trying to think what might help alleviate all this longing, for what? Some impossible imagined state perhaps somehow safer and less terrible and unbearably, terrifyingly beautiful than what is before us every minute, from which we cannot look away? It's hopeless and opaque all this, and yet hope pours from it like light. Hope is what it's made of. Life is its own sickness and its cure. It goes on. Going on is what is does endlessly and with such unimaginable power that Death is a joke compared to it. A temporary respite. A fictitious pause. Of which the blind and wordless mind and heart of Life knows nothing.

Douglas Thompson

THE FALLEN WEST

Douglas Thompson was born in Glasgow, Scotland, in 1967 and won the Herald/Grolsch Question Of Style Award in 1989, 2nd prize in the Neil Gunn Writing Competition in 2007, and the Faith/Unbelief Poetry Prize in 2016. His short stories and poems have appeared in a wide range of magazines and anthologies, including Ambit, New Writing Scotland and Albedo One.

His website is at:

https://douglasthompson.wordpress.com/

His novels and collections to date are:

Ultrameta
Sylvow
Apoidea
Mechagnosis
Entanglement
The Rhymer
The Brahan Seer
Volwys & Other Stories
The Sleep Corporation
Barking Circus
Eternity's Windfall

DOUGLAS THOMPSON

THE FALLEN WEST

THIS IS A SNUGGLY BOOK

ISBN: 978-1-943813-55-1

CONTENTS

THE FALLEN WEST

BRIGHT NOVEMBER

I who am so sane and safe in my commuter suit. I keep it together, just, for most of the year. Subdued by the daily anaesthetic rhythms, train on rails, shiny shoes on tarmacadam. Maybe my suit knows what it's all for. It certainly seems to know where it's going. Perhaps I should ask it. But it has so few controls. Perhaps the suit I mean now is the one of flesh rather than the one of tweed and silk. The one with the clockwork heart and the oh so jaded eyes, misted as grimy windows that were once, I do flatter myself to believe, polished and gleaming as bright diamonds that lit up the mournful dark of human habit and self-doubt. But those days are passed, I am the lobotomised robotic now, hypnotic, neurotic. Fractured, numbed by the scars and bruises, my memory of my collision with Kyrie, my forbidden beloved. My secret mistress who raised my spirit above the clouds then dashed it on the mean damp earth a hundred miles below. Most of the year I can almost forget her, for whole hours on end. Or maybe only fifteen-minute intervals, but that is still pretty good, believe me. Forget her, nearly mostly, until November comes around. That haunted season when I first met her. And the light then, it's all about the light. It has that sweetly tired and yellowed quality to it as the year's end looms. That light and that season seize me every time, and I am lost again. And then I must skirt furtively away and catch a train once more to her side of the city, the Southside, *Mirrorworld* as we called it. South of the river, where everything was upside down and we walked and talked backwards, our moral order inverted.

These days I've found some shortcuts. The easiest one is through frozen puddles, if the frost has come early. One simply has to look around to check the street is quiet and nobody is peering out from their net curtains, then smash the ice up into a few jagged fragments with your umbrella tip. Then bend down and lift up a jagged edge or two, take a deep breath and leap down and into the darkness underneath. One passes through that momentary shade as if blinking, or fainting, enduring a little death in the thoroughly French sense then abracadabra: you find yourself falling out and upwards and backwards into a similar but different street in Mirrorworld. Shall we go there now, today? I have much to show you, none of which you'll understand, which is of course how you like it. Mirrorworld these days has become my personal museum of Kyrie, haunted by my memories of her, by her own stories of her past, by shadows and glimpses of her friends and relatives, all aged and changed and moved on. Everyone has moved on except me. I am trapped in Mirrorworld essentially, or addicted to it at least, like a high-class drug for rich decadents. I keep coming back for more, and am progressively depraved and degraded by the experience, or artistically uplifted, depending on your viewpoint. Just when does a sad stalker become a creative genius? The day he finally sculpts all his longing into a golden statue of course, and everybody sees at last what he was getting at and confess that they would have worshipped her too. Mirrorworld is Kyrie's living tomb, her cenotaph and autograph. So many fragments play there, simultaneously, out of time and out of tune. And now you must wander through them with me, arm in arm and hand in hand.

Look, here is her street. Brush that puddle-ice off your coat there. Walking backwards a little difficult for you? You'll find it easier after a while. Human societies are like that after all, if enough of you do the absurd, anything really, it soon becomes quite normal and natural and commonplace. It's going back you have to watch. When you return to the north side of the river you'll think everyone is upside down there.

I love her street. The buildings are a strange disparate mixture of scales and styles and periods, all slightly shabby in that Southside seen-better-days sort of way. The golden Victorian or Georgian era, that fit of optimism in which they were conceived and constructed: long since passed. Her flat is guarded by her two daughters Phoebe and Demetra. One has the head of a lioness, the other the beak, talons, feathers and wings of an eagle. No, these are not metaphors. In Mirrorworld all metaphors are manifest, that's one of the rules you'll learn as we go along. I walk up the little pathway through her garden from the street and knock once more on the old painted door, just as I did so many times that winter long ago with my heart in my mouth like a lovesick boy. The echo of that doorknob booms into eternity like grey and dismal waves inside some remote cave off the North Sea, before the door creaks open. Once, it would have been Kyrie herself with that enigmatic expression of part-excited love, part-resentment for my having made her love me, part-doom at knowing there could be no possible happy ending to such a saga involving a married man like me. A north-side refugee robot with clockwork heart ticking in his shirt with all the menace of a commuter-train nail bomb. But today it is Phoebe who answers and instead of speech issues the roar of a lioness, a great rolling purr of sound that rattles the pebbles in her rockery and makes my bones vibrate like reedy bamboo flutes.

The door is duly opened with desultory disregard and I am permitted to enter, closing it shut behind me, then following Phoebe's dispassionate back towards the steps down to the basement. Before we can descend however, Demetra emerges from her bedroom and flies into the air in the hall above us, to peck and tear at my face and shoulders while screeching wildly. Many of her bluish white feathers are dislodged in the process of this unseemly fracas, and left to see-saw down to the floor in that mellifluously weightless way that feathers do. The altercation is terminated by Phoebe turning her furry head around and half-heartedly snapping her jaws at her unruly avian sister. On the way down the stairs I am strangely touched to notice this detail: that Phoebe is barefoot today and in fact has delicate little tawny-coloured lion paws whose nails make clipping sounds against the stone surface of the steps.

Ah, what a scene awaits us. This was once the kitchen, with a door onto the sunny backcourt filled with fragments of ruined buildings, the kitchen where Kyrie and I first sat together one autumn morning and I told her how beautiful she was and our love began its slow spiralling descent into magnificent madness. But today, as it always is with the insane internal logic of dreams, the space has been entirely re-organised and displaced in space and time to resemble a small swimming pool, six-feet deep in clear blue water reeking antiseptically of chlorine, at the bottom of which Kyrie herself sits in an armchair in a diving suit, weighted down by heavy metal clogs, reading the morning's newspaper through the thick glass visor of her diving helmet. I strip to my underpants and dip beneath the water to swim towards her, gesticulating wildly to try and gain her attention as clouds of bubbles progressively leak from my mouth and stream skywards like migrating swifts. Getting closer and looking through her visor glass I can see that she has several shoals of little fish, minnows and sticklebacks, swimming around in there in front of her face like idle thoughts.

She smiles sweetly as she recognises me and I am greatly heartened to see her put down her newspaper and reach up to grasp the iron bolts either side of her visor and unfasten it. Swinging open the glass, large transparent bubbles of fresh air pop outwards in quick succession, each expanding like hot air balloons until the pressure in the room gets too intense and the windows shatter and water begins spewing out over the windowsills and into the garden. I grab an air bubble and jostle around inside it, talking to her as best I can in fits and bursts until the barometric chaos subsides. She takes her helmet off with a sharp turn to the left, then steps out of the diving suit whose masculinity-masking-femininity is oddly arousing in a Matryoshka doll sort of way. *Bruce, Bruce, I always knew you would come back . . .* she laughs childishly, each musical note spinning across the room like machine-gun fire, amid the spinning diadems of autumn light on retreating water.

Really? You had an odd way of showing it then. By which I mean telling me you'd call the police if I ever contacted you again. Just what kind of a come-on is that supposed to be?

None whatsoever of course, she smiles. *You're a complete weirdo shitbag and I meant it when I said it, but everything's different now.*

Is it? —I ask sceptically, but looking around to observe again the progressively draining kettle of a room, have to concede that my objection is ill-founded. *I guess we're dead or this is some whacky dream, but I must say it's nice to see you up-close again and with a happy expression on your lovely face, as opposed to passing me on the street with your head down pretending we never happened. Your hair, your ears, your eyes. Your lovely girlish knees, how nice to see those again and know that them and you are still connected happily together.*

That's sweet of you, she says, *in a bonkers sort of way, you always were sweet and kind, even though you were shagging me at the same time as your wife and God knows how many others.*

Not true, there were no others . . . I begin to correct but she interjects energetically:

Enough, no more wind and prattle. That's where we went wrong last time. I see that the water, the collected rain of a hundred winter nights without you, is all draining away now. You're standing there in your underpants so we best change clothes and scenes before I contemplate doing dirty things with you like we used to. What do you say?

16

With a sweep of her lovely long-fingered hand, Kyrie wipes the water-damaged room aside and dresses us both in long flowing cloaks woven out of multi-coloured autumn leaves and takes us for a stroll in nearby Queen's Park. Which Queen precisely I rarely stopped to ponder when we were together. Snow Queen, Queen of Sheba. Today the myriad colours and textures of our patchwork cloaks are most astounding. Indeed, they are far from static objects obeying the laws of known physics. Each leaf is wont to change at any moment, flickering like a television screen, to reveal distant views of pine forests and sunsets, places perhaps where Kyrie and I wandered once on our secret stolen hours together, falling for each other and struggling not to, in turn, like restless sleepers, drinkers of salt water dying of thirst.

It is so beautiful today again . . . Kyrie sighs, *like November, those magical days and evenings we shared.*

You're reading my mind, I answer. *They'll never die, will they? We'll always keep coming back here in our memories and dreams. Like ghosts. We are ghosts already in a way, aren't we?*

As if to answer me eloquently, she turns, takes my hand then walks right through me until her head is looking out the back of mine. I must say that it's an entirely new and rather spectacular experience. It makes me tingle all over, sort of like sex but without the sequence or climax, without the mess or the grunting, the beginning or the ending. No form of guilt or tissue paper is remotely required. *That was nice, thanks.* I say as we pull away.

Yes, look . . . she says as we keep walking and rotating around a few pathways approaching the top of the park, the little hillock with the flagpole and the spectacular view north to the rest of the city languishing in yellow evening light. *How did it get round to evening again?*

It always does, I say, taking her hand once more, and trying not to slip right through her. *That's one of the trademarks of Mirrorworld. It's always November and it always becomes evening and sunset ridiculously soon. The whole of nature acts as an enormous melodramatic poetic background fixated on metaphors for decay and death.*

Oh, that sounds so sad and morbid. Kyrie smiles that childlike, slightly unhinged smile of hers, eyes crazed as they always were with the madness of unwise attraction. *We weren't about death were we? I felt we were about life and light, potential, the paths not taken, the chance to do something wild, burn bright like shooting stars before we had to fizzle out and retire wounded into the darkness of old-age and incontinence.*

A stickler for words, it occurs to me that incontinence, using the strictest definition, was very much our problem, but keep schtum. *I think I see at last,* I laugh aloud, *what we were, what we were for. Something to light up the darkness, to light the way* . . . home, I nearly add but stop myself. She inhales sharply, having read my mind anyway it seems. Suddenly I am more aware of the oncoming darkness, of the chill, of the frost clinging to every shadowed blade of grass, the whisper of winter in the breeze at our backs.

You have to go again, as ever, don't you? She smiles bravely, but I can see that self-pity in her eyes, the essence of a lost little girl that always made it so hard for me not to love her, not to want to help her. Her father had rejected her. It was like a template, a jigsaw piece, an ever-repeating paradigm. Every man that ever said goodbye, even for an hour, never mind a night or a few days, was repeating that, walking over her grave. I bring her close and kiss her forehead, the most chaste and pure of gestures. My beloved Kyrie, lost forever in space and time.

In the far distance beyond the blackened silhouettes of trees, the patchwork city glistens in yellow light, Victorian grid of tartan tenements and needle steeples. Behind it all the hills, the Campsies and Ben Lomond white with snow, glimmer like ice cubes in a glass of whisky before the whole table top is upended. Another hand, not Kyrie's this time, but someone darker's, sweeps the whole chessboard of the city up, collapses it sideways and draws me through one of its black squares, howling for a second like a reluctant newborn, back towards the north side.

Next day Emily reassembles me as usual from my constituent parts, winds up the spring inside me with a key between my shoulder blades, and sets me loose again, sends me out into the world once more to earn a crust. Tick-tock, click-clack, with the wind at my back, I make my way down through the habitual streets to our suburban train station. But hark, I'd swear that is no ordinary November breeze chilling my neck but the voice of Kyrie sighing as I reach the street corner and whispering into my ear in the frosty morning air *Be Careful*. We are in love you see and love is like this; it makes the customary divisions between Mirrorworld and the ordinary world of everyday boredom surprisingly weak and malleable. Somehow she is watching me wherever I go. Fantasising about me every night, so she tells me, as she caresses herself with her long elegant fingers. Closing her fluttering eyelids she is able to divine my location remotely, find me wheresoever I may be in the world and watch me like some disembodied eye. This is why I see her as all those blood-red suns and ghostly white full moons, those sailing orbs that soar above me as I pace this winter city and its surrounding countryside, trying to sort myself out, trying not to have an affair with Kyrie. But the eye is vertical as well as horizontal. The fissure of sunset through clouds is also the memory of her beloved little sex, engorged, enflamed red jewel adrift amid the sea of silken pink flesh of her thighs as she kneels over me, giggling. Mirrorworld you see, top to tail, all metaphors are manifest. She and I are the meeting of north and south, dark and light, not just man and woman.

But what am I saying? I'm talking as if all this business is still going on when I've already explained that it's all over. But I'm not so sure anymore, increasingly uncertain. What actual existence has love after all, other than inside our own heads? How strange that is, for something so dominant in our lives. How far-fetched the leap of faith, our trust that the object of our desire dreams of us equally in a shared hallucination, or dreams at all. I resolve to go on loving Kyrie, even though she renounced us and pronounced me persona non grata. I go on loving within the kingdom of my own head, and who is to stop me? And thus Kyrie lives on, in my heart and mind and in these pages. I try to get on with the everyday, to conduct my life normally, but once opened: the windows and doors to Mirrorworld cannot be closed so easily. Indeed, I even know how to make my own, I carry them with me.

I disembark when my train arrives at the city centre, jostled by the crowd of other eager robots, and commence my routine walk up Sauchiehall Street. Rather than arrive at my office today, I take a detour through the West End Park instead and a find a quiet corner between two glossy-leafed rhododendrons in which to unfold a hinged black wooden frame from inside my briefcase. A tricky trapezoid, rapid rhomboid, parallelogramophone of forbidden music, the frames rotate to form a right-angled rectangle and then I simply step through it once like a little girl with her skipping rope or hula hoop. Ka-boom! I vanish sideways out of our world, condense into a straight line of carbon shadow in flatland stripped of my higher dimensions, then disperse as dust on the wind, a slate wiped clean.

I fall out of the sky above Queen's Park and land laughing in a duck pond. I can tell immediately that I am back in never-time again, a years-ago November, before the whole thing got too serious. When Kyrie and I could still just about convince ourselves we were only friends. Friends who kissed a lot and licked each other's genitals. As you do. I shake myself dry as best I can, but am chilling fast in the morning air. Clouds of fog still cling to the dips and hollows of the park as I hurry my way along the manicured curving paths over the hill towards Kyrie's district. She receives me shivering at her door. Her guardian daughters, twin moons of caution and prudence, are both absent today, drawn south by the gravitational pull of London. Only I really need to get out of my damp clothes, but she gets out of hers also, obligingly mirroring to the last, and we sink together into each end of a steaming hot bath, to discuss life, love and the universe as usual. Her hair is tied up behind her head in a most appealing tortoise-shell clasp, revealing her charming little ears. She smiles mischievously.

What the hell are we going to do . . . ? —I sigh. *Emily still suspects nothing.*

But we can't go on like this, Kyrie nods sagely, *all this surreptitious skulduggery goes completely against my moral order. It occurred to me the other day that perhaps you were thoroughly mad and you've somehow drawn me into a kind of communal madness with you. I mean, we've hardly known each other more than a handful of weeks. How long has it been exactly?*

About twelve years . . . I calculate.

Her brow furrows. *Are we dead, Bruce? One loses track of time in the afterlife.*

Quite possibly, I agree. *I always said that breaking up would be like that for us. That we would be dead people for the rest of our lives, robots going through the motions.*

But was there really ever any other way?

To have confessed to Emily then left her, I suppose. I was ready to do it, but you stopped me, remember?

You stopped yourself if you really think about it, but tell you what: let's not really think about it. She pours me a cup of tea from a little china teapot she's brought to the bath's edge specially, sitting on a tray on the bathroom floor. All very genteel. *Do you think there are actually choices in life? Parallel universes even, of theoretically infinite number, in which we each did things differently and life went on in a completely different way?*

No, in a word. I answer bluntly. *That's a load of mystical bollocks that particle physicists have dreamed up recently, but it feels to me as if it has no basis whatsoever in real life as we experience it. Just goes to show that our scientists have become merely priests, and science our religion.*

You favour the idea of karma then?

Yes, the inevitability of a pre-destined future that is a product of who we each are. Time is circular.

But you mention God quite a lot, you know, and not just at the top of your voice when you're having orgasms with me. What's that all about?

I suppose I find him or it a useful thought experiment, or maybe just an atavistic paradigm which I can't shake off, along with a lot of other baggage from my parents. I can accept him as a metaphor, more of a her than a him, for the spirit of all life on this planet. Gaia, if you will.

But that's not a very reasonable or moral god or goddess really is it? She muses.

No, indeed, and neither are you . . . I smile sadly and she leans forward from her side of the bath and kisses me passionately on the lips. I run my hand across the marvellously soft and smooth skin of her back and arms and legs, like strawberry sorbet I sometimes think, as if scarcely there at all, the mellifluous epidermis of her boundary with the outer world, melt-in-the-mouth sweetness of oestrogen. Just where does Kyrie end, if she ends at all? She is a breeze, a mist, a breaking wave. And the bathroom is filling with fog now, as she runs in more hot water. I lose sight of her and when my vision clears I find we are walking hand in hand a few blocks away, in our long winter coats and hats, down by a bend in the River Cart, looking up at the windows of a rented flat I once planned to share with her. This district is cold and grey, too few gardens, too many tall tenements in narrow streets.

What were we thinking of? —She chuckles, looping her arm through mine in a gesture I always loved, thinking it made me feel strong and reliable and useful.

You had a house, but you never seemed at home in it. I wonder how much time you might have spent round here instead if I had gone ahead with this? —I ask her.

The dampness in the walls . . . She begins, *the dry rot, the spores, the mushrooms . . .*

Nah, let's be honest, Kyrie, the wood rot was in just one room that you never used. It was more than that. That house oppressed you. You claimed you couldn't get peace when Phoebe and Demetra were home with their friends round, but we both know that didn't happen much. You were most oppressed of all when the two of them were absent and you were left alone in the place. That was when you felt the strongest urge of all to leap into your campervan and speed around the city and the country, escaping yourself, shadow-boxing some inner demon, pursuing some elusive sense of freedom and happiness.

And isn't it elusive for all of us? She counters.

Yes, I concede. *But for you more than most. It was the departure of John and all his children that made that house too quiet for you to bear, I reckon. A big family like the one you grew up in. Your father left you, and then years later there was John leaving you too, taking his kids with him, repeating the paradigm but worse this time, leaving you only your daughters. You still have feelings for him. You dated me, if one might use such a quaint term for an adulterous bastard like me, on the rebound.*

24

Kyrie tenses, stiffens and drops my hand and now I know I've gone too far. *Here you go again! Haven't you learned diddley-squat? This is what I grew to hate about you, the way you always tried to psychoanalyse me!*

But I love you. Isn't it inevitable to want to try to understand those we love?

But you don't understand at all. You misunderstand. You disregard my own explanations for myself with obscene arrogance, as if you know, as if you have lived my life when in fact only I have. Only I know the truth about me. You patronise me. I don't want to be understood, not by you at any rate. You're not fit to understand me! She is raging now, eyes blazing, come to a standstill on a street corner, as the river mist thickens, comes pouring up the street like a prowling cat.

I lose her again in the grey fog of confusion, mutual miscomprehension. Except for her beloved voice, that gentle almost-whispering tone so burned into my memory which pursues me as ever, echoing down the street in the muffling fog, wrapping itself around me like a scarf, like a hangman's noose: *I don't want to be understood.* A self-fulfilling prophecy.

So now I am left alone again. The mist half clears and I find I am seated in Café Tapioca on Pollokshaws Road, where Kyrie and I met so many times, with all the midweek traffic lurching by outside, except that the place is nearly empty, oddly cold, and filled with the sort of winter mist that only belongs outside on street corners. You'd think it would set off the fire alarm. Two middle-aged women are seated at a nearby table eating gateau with forks, but one of them is wearing a Halloween mask of a skull, and continuing to talk and sip tea as if everything is normal. A young man is sitting at another table near the windows onto the street, scribbling rapidly into a notebook, as if writing poetry. He looks up and I see he has the face of an old-fashioned clock, complete with Roman numerals and hour and minute hands decorated like florid spears.

The waitress comes over to serve me, and I remember her sadly beautiful face from years ago, sense that she recognises and remembers me. She is made sadder still by her empathy, her inkling that Kyrie and I are no more and I am a sad sack inhabiting my haunted memories of her. I open up the tall black hardback menu and look for something to order but find only a printed black square on the page which grows and amplifies bringing with it the sound of discordant middle-European music played by a string quintet, as the mist in the café thickens and I begin to cough and choke. The twelve-tone noise and blackness overtakes everything else until I feel a jolt in my stomach, a sudden feeling of falling, and wake up, coughing, back on the north-side.

How are you going to vote in the referendum? —Someone is asking me.

What? Say that again? I repeat, trying to get my breath back.

The Robot Referendum. Whether Robotland should leave the United Kingdom of Great Boredom and weather-is-dire land. I am at work now I see, seated at my computer desk inside my office: the Cutty Sark building, a great swelling attic of distorted sarking boards like ship planks that creak in the wind, tapping away at my computer keys. I search my mind for any opinion on this issue. *I think we should be free,* I say at last, . . . *it's time we took responsibility for ourselves and grew up, like teenagers leaving home, took our freedom.*

My colleague laughs. *How ridiculous! Robots can't run their own affairs! They need real people to run things!*

I smile humbly, deferentially, sadly, to myself. If only I could just be a robot. If only I had never loved, had never fallen for Kyrie. If only I could forget her now. If only I had no secrets, could go on living every day mechanically sustained on clockwork. If only. But my heart is alive, it bleeds as much as that of any human being who has ever loved. Rubble overgrown with ivy, all soaring arches and broken windows, it is a ruined cathedral.

Exhausted, dishevelled, I drag myself up and out of a puddle on a pavement on the north side and sit on the ground with my back against some well-to-do suburban garden fence, trying to get my breath back. Eventually I get to my feet and struggle at length to brush the worst of the muck off my jacket and trousers. I take my pocket watch on its long silver chain from my waistcoat and check the time. The glass is cracked, but the damn hands still hobbling their way around with fiendish persistence. Rushing as ever, as I often did, to get home before my wife Emily so I could sit there and pretend I hadn't been over at Kyrie's all day. I limp, I hobble, a wounded animal who's just had his wounds licked, back up the humpback hills of suburbia towards the immaculate home I share with Emily.

Everything is perfect there, not a speck of dust, not an ornament out of place. I get home breathless, only minutes before her. Not yet out of my winter overcoat and suit when she arrives, Emily comes in and takes these apart for me. I stand in the hall with arms spread wide like a scarecrow as she disassembles me. My arms click off, my chest clicks open, the jaws of my ribcage spreading wide to give up, with only the very slightest of resistance, my clockwork heart ticking away, a miraculous well-oiled piece of Victorian machinery. She lifts it out gingerly and places it on the mantelpiece where we're both sure I won't need it until tomorrow. She takes my legs off and folds them up over a hanger and puts them into our full-height wardrobes in the bedroom. She unscrews my hands and fingers and polishes and dries them each carefully before putting them away in the cutlery drawer in the kitchen. My head gets stored with my feet and boots, under the upholstered footstool in the hallway, lying sideways where its dead eyes can stare endlessly across the deep weave of hall carpet finely groomed as wheat sheaves, towards the awaited spectacle of sweet bright November light that will fall there again, on the distant living room carpet each morning from now until eternity.

Emily switches the television on, and settles down to a long satisfying evening of watching real people.

BREAKS-IT BRITAIN

In Breaks-it Britain, when the scrawny chickens don't come home to roast no more, the yobs and skinhead racists crowd around campfires at night. Amid the rubble of gutted buildings they barbie their own pit bulls on the flames. Singing rousing songs of white supremacy and swigging west-country cider and London gin, laughing about foreigners and how they'll never, ever, let them in.

In Breaks-it Britain the Shard is finally a shard, the Gherkin pickled, the Cheese Grater no longer great, the Walkie-talkie hobbled and silent, for the City suits are all fled, the City bled, like flocks of crows they've all flown south long since to pepper the pavements of Frankfurt and Paris with life-giving Capitalist guano, their trickle-down largesse.

Let us go then you and I, across the million glass fragments of broken windows fallen from the sky, and marvel at the sweet mercy of the London rain which washes the eye of memory and circumvents the brain. And let us believe that all of this was done not just to spite the slimy Frenchman and teach a lesson to the Hun, but to give back shining on a plate to every ordinary working man, and his ordinary working mate, the glorious and glamorous prospect thus to shape his limpid, lumpen fate: of being able to call someone wog or nigger to their uncomprehending face.

Or so the ghost of Saint Theresa was telling me as I followed her across the twilight ruins one Thursday night in early February. Did she have feet? Was she using them? It was hard to see. She just floated and hovered above the ground in something like a long white nightdress and zoomed ahead spookily, progressing through the blighted rubble of such neighbourhoods as Hampstead and Kentish Town with the gusto of an impatient taxi driver of olden times. It all recalled to me nostalgically the blithe and plucky disregard with which she had ignored all the checks and balances of our dying democracy culminating in a mob lynching her and hanging her from a lamppost in Hyde Park. Or so the history picture books told us when we were young anyway. Before we burned all the books.

Just before Camden Locks I chanced upon the Holy Chapel of the Apparition of Thatcher, famously sculpted out of corrugated iron on the exact spot where Saint Theresa reputedly received an ecstatic vision one October morning, while stopping off for a coffee break on the way to Chequers, of the ghost of Thatcher telling her she had a divine mandate to shaft Britain right up the arse with a right royal hard unlubricated Breaks-it. The devout, a raggle-taggle hotpotch of bare-footed pilgrims and defrocked ministers and nuns, were huddled outside in between bouts of marching around it anticlockwise in the manner of muzzies at Mecca or weekend shoppers at the ancient temple of Ikea looking for parking spaces.

Not that parking or cars are a problem for anyone

anymore. At Camden I looked down into the long-clogged-up Regents Canal where the rusting car rustlers and stevedores were, as usual, using long poles, in the manner of Venetian gondoliers, to manoeuvre the enormous clanging river of wrecked automobiles eastwards around Kings Cross and Shoreditch towards Limehouse Docks where the blowtorches blaze night and day to release scrap metal for the near-penniless to buy meagre meals with. But this is England. The stevedores sing obscene songs in hearty voices as they jump across the canal, bouncing gaily from car bonnet to bumper and crushed metal roof to towpath. It makes for a party atmosphere, even on rainy days which are many.

In Leicester Square I watched the ghostly signs and broken lights, the old posters for big movie shows and extravaganzas of a former age of pomp and romp and all that jazz. A light drizzle was falling and I hid in a boarded-up shop entrance as a pack of dogs howled by, pursuing a whimpering vagrant in torn rags running on all fours, his arse on fire, being pelted by dirty-faced children lobbing colourful pieces of viciously-configured Lego at him. Some old vestige of electrical huff-puff must have momentarily ghosted into life, because as I lifted my eyes to the grey-tinged clouds, some sign thingy flickered on and off: Burgher King flashed across The Prince Of Whales and the Drome Of Hippos, and stirred a vague memory of some old history lesson of how it had meant something, but I scratched my head and failed to draw out any more of it. Some kind of circus maybe, run by royal folks who danced on animals and every geezer worshipped. But no, it was gone, long gone.

Then it seemed to me that pesky white ghost of Theresa appeared again of a moment, walking, skipping through shop windows and through the endlessly- reflected arrays of unreachable café tables thick with dust, beckoning me down into the placed marked U-Ground, and I was loathe to follow. Down many steps I found reeking crowds in the dark laid out along platforms like battle-weary soldiers. I was drawn by the smell of meat on spits, but the men tending them were set like bulldogs, prodding me off with pitchforks and cattlebrands, and more I looked in the gloom the less I liked what I saw of the kind of the game they were roasting. One of them called after me as I fled, taunting: *Strange friend, here is no cause to retch, men will go content with what we spoiled . . . whatever hope was yours I butchered also.*

In the square of the Trafalgar, I saw Red Routemaster buses piled high in a twisted tangle like dancing witches frozen freeze-frame, wrapped around Nelson's column like so many gargantuan bronteysauri sisters, bones of drone-like megafauna. I found black stone lions and a fountain clogged with foul fowl slime, the bones and feathers of a million feasted-upon pigeons, broad steps and tall columns marvellously fluted and topped with all manner of fruit and vedge carved of stone which I wished were real and I might have shimmied up to pluck and bring them downwards like luscious grapes or them bent Brit bananas whot Johnny Europe once tried to straighten but old bulldog Churchill showed 'em not. In the distance, between a valley of gutted facades I spied the spire of Big Ben all coggled and sprung open like a busted bedside alarm clock that had clucked and rattled its last warning. The ghost of them olde wheezers beneath it slumbered on, their time for tittle-tattle and tommy-rot gone.

I kept going south, weary of foot and spirit. In the ruins of Saint Paul's I found the last followers of the true inner sect of Saint Theresa, all dressed in white robes, kneeling in prayer beneath the fragmented dome, through which could be seen bright fragments of blue sky and wind-torn passing clouds. It was all very last resort Rosetti, very Burne-down-Jones. *There'll always be an England,* they sang, *full of all things white and beautiful, with Tornados bending near the earth to drop their bombs of gold.* Feeling suddenly sick with hunger, I staggered out onto the banks of mother Thames where I could lie on my side double up with my knees under my chin recounting some half-remembered gibberish about dirty fingernails and Margate sands. The Thames was foggy, like a big yellow dog was pish-splashing around in it making it into an incomprehensible Turner and sniffing his big soft snout like a mythical coke addict, glue-sniffer more like. I wanted to cross yon funny once-moderne bridge towards that Banksy's Backside PowerStation thing which I'd probably dreamt had been an art gallery once, but all the tension members and jiggy-jaggy bits had burst and sprung long since, showering the once-proud capital with shrapnel like so many of Agincourt's arrows.

I found a boat instead, forged by hand by a bored former-artisan from the remnants of the hide of a taxidermied elephant stolen from something called once the Victoria & Albert. I rowed and rowed but drifted and was drawn off course, under jiggered London Bridge and past the once-dreaded Tower of Tourists.

To Wapping then I came, burning. I hopped out finally at Greenwich and it's ruined observatory which I recalled hearing was once the centre of the whole world and the zero-point of conquered time. But time had proved a wild old beast it seemed, a bucking bronco that had thrown every cunt in the end. I sat in the park among the long grass and munched on a few diseased pigeons stolen from a fox burrow, a king's banquet by any current standards. Across the way, above the scattered lights of twilight bonfires, the fading sunset lit up the tarnished jewel of the old Canary Tower, its splintered pyramidal top raided as by Egyptian tomb-raiders of old, from which the little yellow birds had vented. I had heard their songs had been well nice once, and simple people had kept pet specimens in cages all across the land to serenade them after a hard day's labouring at many small things of modest satisfaction. I grew nostalgic remembering crazy old stories like that which my old man used to tell me. Sometimes in the old days I'd fall asleep imagining them golden canaries and their pretty little songs and what they might have sounded off like.

I woke sometime after midnight with a fox at my throat who I shook off after a hearty struggle, laughing. Only come sunrise when the frost chill waned did I tumble that he'd gone off with three of my fingers like a butcher's sausages. Well thems the breaks, I says to meself, it's all about trade this life after all, give and take along the way until your luck runs out and the big man, or mam, upstairs asks to see you.

THE TWELVE SEASONS

1
January

Toe and boot
underfoot
crunch and slither
ice and frost
snow falls forever
glimmer sparkle
amid the dark until
at last the stars themselves
not lost, aglow as though they
have been brought down, reversed
the universe itself upended
the blackness of space freezing
fills my veins and eases the pulse
towards eternity's slow turn
of Catherine wheels of galaxies
all life suspended, look
at that which does not live
can at least no longer die
I fall, cry out, lose my grip
grapple, topple, slip and dip

lose consciousness
and on my back, upended
find sleep, perfection
my face a landscape
sculpted by lost memory
scoured by winds
forgotten by light
as life abates
turns tides
and seeds abide
and wait.

2
February

Watercolour sunrise paints itself
glimpsed through my curtains
waking from the torpor of
a dream of lost youth
some bitter message from
Morpheus, Hypnos, Nyx
the dream gods, about how
I have never fitted anywhere
nor cared for people much
the ever-optimistic birds chirping
out there, as if they can pull-off
this illegally early spring
without the grey wardens
of Presbyterian boredom
apprehending them under the terms
of the curtailment of fun and laughter act
good luck to them I say go little guys
the crows survey the street
like passing dive bombers
strafing us with their wry

laughs of ancient cynicism
building nests already
from all that wreckage of blasted branches
strewn by the January gales
everything is opportunity
a new Jerusalem in every Babel
only trust in it, Life whispers
part those curtains, embrace light
spread those dusty wings, take flight
take risks, let winter's chill lick clean
your wounds and heal and build
as all beginnings might.

3
March

March is the month that birthed me
the year's start in ancient times
when war and farming resumed
the encyclopaedia tells us
without apparent irony as if
such happy pursuits have long been
humanity's sport and always will be
conflict and building, a fair summation
of my lot upon this earth
intertwined: destruction and creation
love, its planting, and its dearth.
And Caesar's reckoning too
those portentous ides, he mocked his seer
ignored the whispers in his burning ear
and paid the price, sunk beneath the tides
of time. There is no crime fate recognises
save blindness to the forces of the coming year.
Like he, I should consent to go as I have come
with flowers budding and birds singing
do not resist, amidst a feast for eye and ear
blood spilt and church bells ringing.

4
April

In a single week
Spring springs in Glasgow
a leaping Jock-in-the-box
a dance of veils
the brittle whalebone filigree
of kohl-black branches
suddenly cloaked in spreading fans
green silk feathers flickering teasingly
amid the pom-poms of candy-floss blossom
bobbing on the breeze of promise
the lithe branches bend, coquettish
the sap rising to the overture of birdsong
recalling every childhood summer
the first remembered whispering
of the rest to come.

5
May

The wisps of cloud above
whipped to cappuccino froth
sighing in the endless drink of blue
all human drama dissolves
the sun become our heartbeat
boiling off irksome mirages
stale excess of time and angst
The garden erupts into colour
invention, fronds, stamens, sepals
architecture of a million alien worlds
enacted here as one. All sing and strain
as does the robin and her mate, ferrying
endless flies and moths into the ivy to feed
the cacophony of new mouths
Onto my page as I write insects drop
life is profligate, ardent, clamouring
effulgent, dare we say almost too much
driven urgently by need and love as am I
by questions such as what queer crop
are human minds required to raise
to serve the sky above.

6
June

Summer in Scotland
the melancholy comfort of rain
listen to the incessant kissing of rooftops
glistening, the sizzling swish of passing cars
let us don the dayglow cagoules of nostalgia
and traipse through muddy fields again
with those long dead who loved and raised us
bravely endured our tantrums and wails
and taught us patience on blighted holidays
the value of keeping going as they did
step by step, year by year, as we must now too
whatever the weather, the mistakes, the regret
knowing that for every sun there is a price to pay
in sweat and burn and consequences
for each unwitting sin:
the belated rain of forgiveness.

7
July

Scintillating brightness of light
white on the green leaves throwing
swaying shadows on walls as wordless mimes
for none but the early birds like me to see
who lick the quiet streets with sandaled feet
savouring the silence and coolness of dawn
the blue a pristine dome above, sacred
we move in pilgrimage as ants upon this earth
who understand Nature's urgency
the sun's brassy fanfare announcing
all the molten gold to come this day
a whole eternity to a butterfly also
a priceless chance to us each instant
if we can just grasp in our clumsy hands
what each tiny thing knows in the core
of its bones and sings of endlessly even
as it offers up its everything
to be burned in joyous sacrifice knowing
from death comes life from shadow light
from forgetting of regret, of risk of pain
of self-consciousness, our very selves:
enlightenment.

8
August

Glasgow has been cut around
by a buzz-saw and towed south
and moored next to Barcelona
Suddenly we have café life
hot mornings where we might
actually seek out the cool of shadows
in which to sip a cappuccino
And we have our Dalis and Miros:
The maddies stripped to the waist
who suddenly emerge white-butterfly-like
after nine months gestation in drink
and drugs rehab and homeless hostels
toothless and disorientated, staggering
and staggered by the unexpected sunshine
wheeling and cawing like wizened crows
shouting what the fuck on street corners
they speak for all of us.

9
September

As if light itself can grow weary
burn out from over-use
too much laughter bring reflective tears
remembered childhood's endless holidays
seep out as fading photographs
into cold new terms and sober uniforms
see now the subtle yellowing in the sky
the grandeur of summer's glorious
oncoming death expressed in symphonies
of cirrostratus armies falling tier on flank
upon their swords of melancholy light
no season takes our breath like autumn
nor expresses better our human plight
who begin our slow cascades of cell decay
before even twenty years of youth
have held their sway, so now we see
our misting breath and frost encroach
as warnings of fragility, senility
here is the beauty so well expressed
across the canvas of the very sky

that what we feel in life
is too precious and ingenious
for any God to let it die, have faith
that all that we must lose, have lost
love and friendship, the hopeless cost
is colour, texture of the leaves that fall
to feed new life wherein
there is no death at all.

10
October

Under the emergent stars
the long drive over *Clisham*
the sea lochs still as my heart
in blue dusk the winking lights
of hamlets scattered as jewels
who make the night not lonely
but resplendent in this peppered land
where each human life is savoured
to serve an unutterable God
the hymns the music of my Gaelic
companions' voices. My communion
the tears in your eyes *mo chara daor*
as I finish reading to the room.
And on the moors we passed
the Yes-signs and Saltires
sang out, a land blossoming
with hope, even as the leaves fell
from the trees around the castle
the watchmen blind to root and vein
our secret spring.

(—Stornoway, Isle of Lewis, 17.09.14)

47

11
November

Return, return the endless
car wash where the brushes turn
lashes rain upon this screen
whips wind through portals of my brain
autumn winter wipe me clean
as grey clouds queue to shed their load
I turn my head from midst the ritual
punctuations of this humdrum life
to catch high up some glimpse of blue
where wisps of cloud run wild
in antique light of burnished gold
my heart leaps at what memory retains
of our brief dreams of sweet escape
our reckless flight through streets
rendered bright with coloured hopes
as carnival flags defy the grey
a thousand times I wash this soul
my wringing hands to mime dismay
but cannot shift the stain
of you on me, of me on you.

12
December

On encircling hills the army first amasses
snowflake-cold, hard-hearted dressed in white
spyglass ice twinkling the city in their sights
poised to descend with north winds
shrieking orders putting citizens to flight
shutting down their roads, barricading
them in under hats and coats.
A winter dusk's beauty in the city
the window-squares light up:
blue curtain twilight falls
teasing glimpses of a million lives
If God exists how could he bear it?
-Each soul a portal through which
an endless rope of memory runs
promising escape to sky and hope
but into which stardust falls and buries
under blankets of forgetfulness
squandered gifts of priceless souls.
To know even one or two of such
individuals intimately: instantly is

to fall in love and start to die
from the agony of knowledge of it
the impossibility of reaching out
and saving beauty, sadness
for the constellations of eternity
enough to do me in. Come, winter
chill these veins, slow this heart
which having drunk its full
too much now wearies, says:
Freeze me so that I may wake
as someone else in time or vanish
under your obliterating trudge.

OUT OF THE BOX

It took me 35 years to find him. The kid I saw jump from one of the boxes at Glasgow's Apollo in 1979, a daredevil feat that briefly landed him in the limelight with the band he loved. It had taken me 25 of those years just to find out his name. These days Jimmy Jessop lived off the grid, which certainly accounted for some of the tracing difficulties. I'd had to ask around in local pubs in the end, before I found a rough location for him. He didn't just not pay the Poll Tax, or its contemporary incarnation the charmingly named Community Tax, he didn't pay any tax. Fair's fair if you don't vote I suppose. Except technically you can never enter an NHS hospital or use a refuse bin or walk across a municipal park either. When I finally met him however, I would find I doubted if he ever did any of those things. His address officially did not exist, not as a residential flat anyway. It was the upper storey of a former glaziers' showroom, long boarded up, which he had acquired in cash through some relative whose name went on the deeds rather than him. The number, "66b" was pretty much his own (logical) invention, and scrawled on his solid steel door in chalk. I'd sent word ahead through a contact of his in the local pub that I would be calling. Otherwise, legend had it, he

51

would just play dead inside for hours in case you were *The Social* or some other form of dangerous snooper. I wondered what the guy had to hide, or if he was just a common-or-garden whacko.

As I stood on the doorstep and drummed my toes, I found some old punk anthem had wormed its way into my head as I gazed back across the dreary afternoon traffic towards a distant horizon of green hills. Stiff Little Fingers: *They wanna waste my life . . . and they've stolen it away.* I took a few steps back and gazed up at the façade above me. A waste of time of course, no windows to the street, no peepholes, the perfect hideaway for a crazy bird man. I hoped this wouldn't be a waste of time, actually. I had walked right across town from the office, rather than risk trying to park my shiny materialistic sports car among the draconian traffic restrictions of student bedsit land in this district. Returning my eyes to the steel door, I found the tune in my head had transmuted, like some kind of spooky automatic update into something closer to recent: *Save me from the nothing I've become,* by Evanescence. Suddenly, I nearly jumped. Keys were turning at last on the other side of the door.

A LEAP IN THE DARK: OUR EDITOR'S REFLECTIONS ON A PUNK YOUTH

Once upon a time my own editor set me a research challenge as a rookie reporter, after I was foolish enough to tell her my fondest punk concert anecdote. Now that I've finally completed my mission, she is retired and I find myself in her shoes, exactly the kind of establishment figure perhaps, that I considered myself an enemy of, back in the days of punk.

He must have leapt a distance of something between 15 and 20 feet, in order to clutch the enormous fire curtain and continue his sliding trajectory, so as to land like a latter-day Errol Flynn almost in the centre of the stage. The crowd, already in joyous uproar at the live rendition of Nice n' Sleazy, went ballistic. Hugh Cornwell and JJ Burnel to their credit, seeing that neither themselves nor the teenager had been harmed, played on good-naturedly. But the infamous Apollo bouncers took another view, and descended upon their prey like hyenas and ejected him into the alleyway through the backstage fire exit in less than a minute.

What happened next, summarises my enduring memory of punk rock, and forms a defining metaphor for me of what the movement was actually about. JJ Burnel, in many ways the unelected leader of the band, stopped playing, closely followed by Hugh and the others. JJ nodded to Hugh and, seemingly telepathically, they agreed their course of action. Hugh announced into the shocked silence of their discontinued set in that laconic north London accent of his (which to us sounded very John Peel): "That's it. We're not playing another note until that kid gets let back in . . . " And we quickly saw they weren't joking.

The inside of Jimmy's house could not have been imagined in advance. You simply had to see it. Rather than throw out the leftover bric-a-brac from the space's previous incarnation as a shop store (it had been a draper's and God knows what all else before a glazier's), he had kept and incorporated the weirdest of it. Tailor's dummies held up his clothes, such as they were (hardly an extensive wardrobe), their elegant plastic fingers holding coats and shirts aloft. One with a hollowed-out stomach incorporated what he called his "sound system", little more than a reconditioned ghetto blaster from a flea market. His television set (I was surprised he had one) was a black-and-white portable circa 1978, balanced on top of the lower half of an elegant pair of plastic female legs with painted toenails: as if the whole thing might strut off any minute if the news turned boring. A wall of exposed white glazed brick has been spray-painted with elaborate graffiti during some previous period of dereliction and vandalism. On the other walls, he had hung old beat-up oil paintings in elaborate gold frames. Edwardian chests of drawers and armoires lay round about, all charred and smashed to varying degrees. It occurred to me for the first time that perhaps punk had been Britain's answer to Europe's Dada and Surrealism, just 50 years late, and made myself a note to research the concept.

Jimmy's shower seemed to be a hole in the roof which he let rainwater fall through now and again by removing festoons of polythene from above it, into an ancient (and cracked) claw-foot bathtub rescued from a skip. For heat and power he had an industrial gas burner and a mobile generator, both obviously pilfered from building sites. Naked bulbs swung from wires on the ceiling, but now and again one would find a charming or quirky detail: a pair of antlers on the wall, a Victorian hobby-horse in the corner with a batman costume hanging over it, or a trio of wooden ducks flying across the wall. In pride of place over a stolen marble fire surround hung a framed portrait of Margaret Thatcher, with a Hitler moustache drawn on and various pieces of newspaper text papered across her features, *God Save The Queen* style.

The man himself I think I had half-imagined to be wearing punk garb, a ridiculous notion of course. He favoured black jeans these days it seemed, trousers, shirt and jacket, black Doc Martens (a touch of continuation there at least!) and his hair was in long rat-like grey dreadlocks swept back, as his hair receded from the front. Maybe I expected him to smell of tobacco, cheap spirits or worse, but he gave off nothing, neutral like his hidden life, a shadow-man. He laughed nervously but infectiously, like a man who indeed hadn't got out much, an astronaut exiled to his own orbit. But when his darting blue eyes finally met your gaze they pinned you with a certain penetrating insight, as unsettling as it was unexpected.

The Stranglers had come late to punk, being classed almost against their will as part of a movement most of whose exponents were a little younger than themselves, but like all true artists, their heads were thoroughly well-tuned into the zeitgeist of those heady days. Disregard of the young by the old was a declaration of war within the context of punk, and the bulk of the Stranglers fans were young alright, a fact doubtless not lost on the band nor indeed their record company. Police and arrests had followed a recent Stranglers gig in London at which strippers had been deployed on stage. They were not strangers to controversy, but the opposite: eager embracers of it. Silence reigned on stage.

The Apollo would be closed in 1985 and demolished in 1987 after a fire. A blessing in a way. I can still clearly remember the way the entire building shook like a ship when the crowds began stamping the floor in unison. It was a death-trap by anyone's standards. The rats probably wore safety vests. The clever Victorian engineers had certainly designed for many eventualities, but I seriously doubt if the point-loads caused by pogo-ing Doc Martens had been among their considerations.

That night, the foot-stopping and slow-clapping took hold to deafening proportions, and the atmosphere quickly became oppressive. The bouncers were big hard guys, but they were outnumbered by a ratio well-beyond their likely command of arithmetic. They looked worried. They backed away against the fire exits, just in case they might be needing them themselves soon. Remarkably quickly, as if they had been expecting something of this nature (they quite possibly had if they read the music press), police appeared at the rear of the theatre, blocking every aisle. In brilliant and uncanny unison, the entire crowd began to whistle the theme from 'Dixon of Dock Green'. This was very Glasgow: a city where withering and all-levelling ridicule is traditionally the base ingredient of most humour, and proven through long experience to be always mightier than the flick-knife. Sure enough, in no time at all, the backstage fire door was opened, the dishevelled kid located and returned unharmed to the theatre. It was our own little terrorist hostage situation. The insurgents had triumphed.

I sat back and relaxed as best I could, in one of Jimmy's flea-eaten sofas, I recognised it vaguely as something by Le Corbusier, probably tipped by (or nicked from)

an architect's office over the road in Park Circus. I asked him to tell me about his life, not from the start necessarily, but from that night, the night of the long leap in the dark, out of the box and onto centre stage, to the present day. He lit a cigarette and poured me a whisky in a plastic cup, made himself a double.

You liked it then? he smiled wryly, baring an intermittent set of teeth that reminded me of partially demolished tenements, *Ma wee acrobatic feat?*

God, yeah . . . I encouraged him, *It looked dangerous. You could have broken you neck, surely? What the hell made you do it?*

Och, ah wiz oot ma box, man. Been drinking for oors beforehand, and snorting speed. I thought ah wiz superman, invincible, ya ken? Every cunt diz when they're that age. Did you no?

Yeah . . . I nodded, *I suppose, when I was pished, certainly.*

Ma mates an' me hud done a loat o' tree climbin' in all when we were younger . . . I remember that. Daft games we used to play, swingin' aboot in trees, playin' at Tarzan in the woods up behind oor hooses. Did you no?

I shook my ahead. *Not flying through space for 20 feet horizontally, 25 feet vertically. You could have gone into the circus, mate. What did you do?*

After ah left school, like? Jimmy looked shy now suddenly. *Dinnae laugh like, but ah pal o' ma dah's goat me a joab in an accountants furm.*

I laughed.

It wasn't about spitting on old ladies. We were bored with that by the time Punk came around. Just joking. You might find it hard to believe now, but back in seventy-six I had the torn and spray-painted jeans and T-shirts, the safety pins, the spiked hair. Well, when I went to concerts anyway, not when I went to school. I was still in secondary. But my brother and his mates bought all the albums, The Sex Pistols, Crass, The Ruts, The Vibrators, The Clash, The Stranglers. The Stranglers were actually seriously skilled musicians by today's dismal standards. The Clash weren't of course . . . every song on their first album consists of about three chords if I remember correctly, but they must have learned to play as they went along because by their third album (London Calling) they were actually technically talented, not just spirited. That was very much the attraction of punk you see, anyone could have a go, it wasn't about skill and patience, it was about energy and anger. Anger above all. Back to the spitting on old ladies thing: a misconception.

The anger was directed at Thatcher's government, the way it looked from where I grew up anyway. But not just at her and her loathsome cabinet who so closely resembled Hitler's inner circle (Tebbit as Goebbels, the unelected Lord Young as Göring), it was directed also at an entire older generation who seemed to have taken leave of their senses and voted that fascist woman into power. In that sense, Punk was a war between the young and the old, with a real urgency to it that I don't think we've seen before or since. I know there'd been all that hippie stuff in the sixties and seventies, where a youth movement became disenchanted with their parents, but that was milder. Vietnam notwithstanding, flower power had been about your parents being square, about there still being a chance you could convert them if you dropped a pill or two in their coffee. Punk, if it was any kind of a successor to that (though its proponents didn't think in such terms), represented a kind of point of no return. Maybe the constant threat of nuclear annihilation at the hands of the Soviets had played a part in this, wearing us down as we grew up with a television diet of apocalypse and societal breakdown, but our mindset was not that our parents were to be negotiated with; they were to be overthrown. I suppose many of us were attracted to the idea of that overthrow as nothing more than an orgy of mindless violence (when you're a fourteen-year-old male those hold a great appeal), but as the product of a highly political household I also dimly grasped it as a means with which to re-make the world order and re-build our society along different lines.

It seemed that Jimmy, to everyone's surprise (not least himself), had turned out to be a pretty good accountant. Passed his exams, risen through the ranks all through the eighties. So the punk boy that had swung through the air that night like a monkey in his hour of glory, had "sold out" like everyone else, The Pistols, The Damned, and ended up wearing a suit and carrying a briefcase, cosying up to rich clients, hoping that some of it might rub off on himself. Got tired of waiting, doing all his bosses work for them, letting them take the credit. So he'd seen his chance and started his own business, took some of the client's with him. Yeah, his accent and his style had seemed a bit rough and ready for some tastes, but some of the clientele had liked that . . . . a particular kind of clientele. The nightclub owners, the 'respectable' gangsters turned property developers. Self-made men like him. Glasgow excels at producing those kind of business-men. In Edinburgh you might need a good school and a posh voice, but in Glasgow sheer balls can go pretty far. Then a recession had hit. Jimmy seemed to be starting to get tipsy by this part of his story. My sense of time and what particular recession he was referring to was hazy. And his wife left him. Now he began to really unburden himself:

Ahh wiz daft like. It wis ma ain fault. Ah hud a wee daughter, eight year auld, and a wife an a loast the pair o' them. Ma oan fuckin' fault so it wiz. There wiz this crackin' wee burd working fur me, gein' me the eye every day. Ah wisnae a bad lookin' bloke back in those days, ye know, but she was ten years ma junior. Ah right wee shag. Beautiful girl, lang blonde hair, figure like . . . . Jimmy put his bottle down and stood up in order to perform an elaborate mime performance worthy of Marcel Marceau, a flurry of arms and hands outlining sumptuous curves in empty space. Getting into the swing of it, he went over and swept one of his tailor's dummies off her feet and wheeled her around the room while singing some kind of execrable disco number from the late eighties. It wasn't punk at any rate.

He flumped back down into his armchair at last, expelling a cloud of dust and flees from the torn lining at the back of it. *So ya get the picture. You married? You never been tempted yoursel'? JJ Burnel, wasn't he supposed tae huv slept wi' a different burd every night fur a year? Ahh wiz bored as hell wi' the wife by then. No spark left in the thing at all. Just her nippin' ma heid every night, telling me do this and do that aboot the hoose, like I was her wean or somethin'. Reminded me too much o' ma auld dear and the auld man, the way they used to treat me like shite. What ah rebelled against, as a punk. What ah . . . .* He lifted his arms up before him in space and I nodded, getting the metaphor. What he had leapt through space for, trying to escape, to think outside the box.

We goat caught in the end, and ah hud tae leave the wife. She turned ma ain daughter against me. My wee girl. She never forgave her daddy. Never seen her in a' these years. Disnae read ma letters, disnae take ma calls. The bitch o' a wife I could live without, but ma wee girl . . . that hurts like.

Unexpected silence reigned suddenly, and Jimmy stared into space over my shoulder, his eyes glazed. I remembered a Stranglers lyric suddenly: *Broken down TV sits in the corner, picture's standing still, standing still.*

What about the girl you had the affair with? Did you not team up with her? I asked quietly.

Jimmy's eyes slowly came back into focus, until he looked at me perplexed, as if I had only just arrived there. *Aye* —he nodded his head then tilted it to one side as if weighing his life in the scales, adding up sums, making his accounts balance. *For a wee while, until ma money ran oot and the business folded, then nae cunt wanted anythin' to do with me. Come tae think o' it your aboot the first fucker tae gie a shite in fifteen year.*

Anger can be a very positive force you see. Pogo-ing up and down at a Stranglers concert (the dance had the great advantage over all others that anybody could do it well), what you felt in the thick of it was not threat but a great sense of

belonging, of warmth, of being amongst people who shared your passion and anger and were directing it towards exactly the same targets. Punk gave me my first sense of belonging as a teenager, an emotion one feels strangely short of at that age. It also gave my first sense that social change was possible. It was Martin Luther King who said that a riot was the language of the unheard, and in 1977 we were the unheard and punk was our riot.

It's hard to believe now, but in a sense punk did win. Thatcher's Poll Tax was finally defeated, three miserable political terms later, and the woman herself duly dispatched. But by that time, most of the punks were wearing suits and getting married or taking the kids to school, and contemplating nothing more rebellious and dangerous than voting Labour. Steel plants and mines and all kinds of heavy industry were gone forever by then. Thatcher had reshaped us all like little wax voodoo dolls, with or without our permission, made us the stewards of a post-industrial husk of a nation, slippery entrepreneurs and managers where before we might have been craftsmen and grafters. Using the hot air in our lungs rather than our sweat and muscle. Flimsy somehow, no longer solid. It was a pity that Thatcher seemed to escape blame for the bank crash of 2008. It was her denouement really, just a long time in the coming. The moment at which we realised that the entire edifice of our nation's supposed financial strength was built on nothing any stronger than sheer hot air. A mirage, a cheap salesman's empty rhetoric. Nations ought to produce things you see. Make things, real physical things and export them. It's called manufacturing, and it makes useful products out of your natural resources, and that's what any nation's wealth should ultimately rest on. It's as if Britain got the idea from somewhere, back in the eighties, that it could just be the world's manager, a useless *git in a suit that lived off everybody else's efforts while it sailed around pontificating, not really doing any work itself. That's called the financial and services industries. And at the end of the day, bullshitters like that always get caught out. You can probably tell by now that the anger of punk has never left me. I hope it never will.*

The lyric in my head was still running: *Duch of the Terrace never grew up, I hope she never will.* So now this was Jimmy's idea of adventure, and having a good time these days. He had lured me out through one of his many Velux windows, taken me up several rusting fire-escape stairs, and now the two of us sat side by side, perched precariously, legs dangling over the A-Listed ornate stone façade of Charing Cross mansions. His training shoes were kicking a carved angel in the face. He passed me a joint, and after a few puffs of that I found myself sharing his bottle of Italian brandy, swigging it straight from the neck, an incongruous choice of tipple in its ornate circular bottle. The stars were out overhead, the traffic whizzing by, four storeys below in streaks of red and yellow, the first Friday night party-goers parading the streets with their territorial catcalls and overcooked laugher. But soon I was laughing myself, at Jimmy's infectiously anarchic view of the universe. I liked the guy. He was honest. He'd learned the value of that the hard way.

It's all shite, man . . . He marvelled, bottle in hand, eyes wide, shaking his head but grinning like a deranged demon. *Men and women, rich and poor, the whole big fuckin' pantomime. You'd think it mattered. Whazzit say in the old testament? My ma' used to quote it . . . vanity, all is vanity. We take credit fur oorsels and oor so-called achievements but we're ah jist chess pieces, tossed aboot by the gods . . .*

Hubris . . . I said.

Whit? His eyes narrowed, as he drew on his joint.

A good Greek word for it. Pride before a fall.

Sounds like sandwich spread. But yeah . . . he laughed, *Those fucking Greeks eh? Every way you jump they goat there first.*

Jimmy . . . I said, relaxing, leaning back on the slate roof, putting my hands behind my head and trying to find the north star. *Do you ever think your life was a mistake? That you made an error back there somewhere? And that if you'd chosen differently then everything would have turned out better?* I was talking about myself of course, my lost dreams of being a real writer rather than a hack, the moral squalor I sometimes found my office at the centre of, but maybe I should have chosen my words more carefully.

I listened to the long sighs of the traffic, the gentle babbling of the city as I waited for his reply. I thought maybe he was taking a particularly long drag on his joint before he answered. But when I opened my eyes a few moments later, he was gone. I sat up rigid, shook my head, pinched myself, tried to sober up. I'd have heard him go past me if he'd climbed back in through the skylight. Sick suddenly, and shit scared, I edged towards the parapet and looked over. Nothing, no disturbance down below. I looked up and along the roof from side to side, top to bottom. Empty. Silence.

As if Jimmy Jessop had remembered how to fly.

THE HOUSE THAT WASN'T THERE

It was when we sat down to breakfast that morning that it happened: a perplexing occurrence. On Sunday mornings I am used to noticing a difference between my wife's sense of hearing and my own, usually manifest in distant church bells: I can always hear them through the windows and trees whereas she rarely can. But that Sunday it was birdsong, a sudden torrent of high-pitched chirping from somewhere outside, some neighbouring back garden perhaps. But this was mid-January, so it could hardly be a nest of newly-hatched chicks we were hearing. But Amy could hear nothing, on any account. Then, to counter this she said something strange: *Do you know that house you pass on the way to the station, the one covered in ivy?*

I nodded absent-mindedly and let her continue talking for a minute, telling me how she often heard intense bird song from within that house's ivy, before I stopped myself and her in mid-sentence with this realisation: *Wait. No. I've never noticed any house covered in ivy between here and the station. I don't think there is one. Where exactly do you mean?*

She paused and we stared at each other for a moment in mutual incomprehension. The ensuing argument eventually evolved into reference to sketched maps and makeshift diagrams on notepaper, before we gave up, put on our winter overcoats, and headed down the street together to try and clear up this new and unexpected mystery that had broken out between us.

Turning in to Ruskin Avenue, a fresh winter breeze picked up, a flock of starlings whirled overhead in the pale blue sky then changed direction and dropped down to drink from the pavement puddles and dazzle us with the iridescent colours of their oily coats. *There it is there . . .* Amy said, stopping and pointing.

Where? I responded. I could see no house covered in ivy.

She pulled me closer to herself in frustration and then something bizarre happened. At the moment of contact between us, as long as she was touching me, I was able to share her illusion and clearly see the mysterious house covered in ivy. It looked old and out of place in the street, a forgotten leftover from some former age, set back and at a slight angle to the other terraces. I pulled away from her and it disappeared. I put my arm around her again and it popped back into my sight, back into existence.

Amy led me by the hand, up the narrow garden path of cracked and uneven stone slabs towards the front of the house-that-was-not-here. She knocked on the non-existent door, and the impact of her clenched fist upon the wood panelling produced a result that was more than acoustic. I saw splinters of coloured light firing off in every direction. Something gave way inside me, my eyelashes became the fluttering black feathers of magpies, one on each shoulder. Reality crumbled like decaying stonework and the impossible door opened onto a house constructed in the narrow gap between nowhere and oblivion. We were ushered in by a tall man wearing silver face-paint and a long flowing cape of white seagull feathers that fluttered continuously in the slightest breeze. On the wall, I could see elaborate hardwood picture frames which held living crustaceans, giant crabs and crayfish, gesturing, clicking and clacking frantically as I passed. I bent closer to examine one and our host seemed flattered by my curiosity. *These are machines, young man, antediluvian automatons constructed from rusted iron and verdigrised brass . . .* he intoned deeply, and then I noticed that he was actually a dwarf wearing stilts made out of whalebone. —*Do you like them?*

I made the mistake here of letting go of Amy's hand for a moment, and found myself back in our normal reality, except that I was now impaled halfway through a brick chimney pot on a nearby rooftop. The pain was excruciating. I could scarcely find the breath and strength to call out for help but I must have managed a scream. She found my hand and held it again and I was transposed instantly back to the house that was nowhere and the company of our most peculiar host.

He ushered us into his equally strange living room and gestured to us to sit down on his armchairs, each of which seemed to have been crafted from some large taxidermied mammals with long dark brown hair, their head and claws lost and distorted somewhere out of sight behind the seat backs. The dwarf himself sat on a small stool with his back to the roaring flames of his fireplace. He donned a carved and painted mask of a puffin's head and began to hold forth as follows:

Don't be afraid of having found this place. This annex always exists, is always open to humanity, or the lost ones at least, the disheartened, the disillusioned. I am the sublime quartermaster of the grainstore of dreams, gardener of lost Eden, guardian of the charnel-house of doomed utopias and impossible yesterdays. Is there anything in particular I can help you with?

I tried to speak, but some unexpected obstruction seemed to be preventing my mouth from releasing speech. Seemingly understanding this, the dwarf handed to Amy and myself colourful and elaborately woven napkins, almost mini-tapestries, which he indicated that we were supposed to hold over our mouths as we spoke. This we did in turn, and found that our words, although intelligible, turned instantly into polished golden balls and small fluttering golden birds which floated about the room above our heads, gradually migrating towards their own sizzling destruction in the fireplace, with much the same falling motion as snow flakes inside a paperweight.

What's happened to the world recently? Amy asked. *We seem to be heading backwards towards war and barbarism. Is there any hope?*

There is nothing but hope, hope is life . . . the dwarf answered, crossing his legs and nodding like a sage. *You are too caught up in the dip and peaks and waves of time to see the bigger pattern. Your short lives rarely allow a glimpse across the true ocean of time. Unlike mine.*

How old are you then? Amy asked, expelling a beautiful gold globe from her face napkin, which bounced across the room twice, sprouted wings, turned into a black-naped oriole then shot into the fire with a satisfying sizzling sound, releasing a pleasing smell of chestnuts.

Oh, I lost count at twenty-thousand years, he chuckled. It was my turn to ask a question or two and I was determined not to waste it. *Will humankind survive into the future?* —I blurted out. *Will people get smarter and stupidity gradually die out? Are there other intelligent life forms out there in the universe and were they all as stupid and cruel as us along the way? Will we ever get to meet them?*

You already know the answers deep down or you would not ask these questions, he answered, a sing-song note of joy entering his intonation. *Time is running backwards. You've already met the aliens and they are part of you. The octopus for instance, is not from earth. All life is degenerating fragments of the death of God, but running in reverse, therefore, the opposite, is happening, which is good news of which you are certainly in need right now by the sound of things. But relax. Enjoy the mayhem. Kill each other while it's still street legal. The future's dull as hell, take it from me, but safe and terribly beautiful. You wouldn't believe the trade in adventure package holidays back to this century by bored futuros. They think you savages are all so authentic, you know.*

Inspired perhaps by the stupefying effect of his extraordinary words upon us, the dwarf led us out into his kitchen, where three circular hatches had been cut into the black-and-white chequer pattern of its vinyl floor, portholes ready and waiting, with the top of white ladders sticking up through them. At his insistence we climbed onto one each and began to descend through the floor. Immediately wind began howling across our bodies and faces as we found ourselves about a thousand feet in the air, the whole town laid out below us. I looked at Amy and we laughed in insane exhilaration. The white ladders, although apparently made of timber, seemed to be of infinite length and strength. I wondered what we would find down there. This town or a subtly altered one? One with or without the house that wasn't really here? Above us, we could see the underside of the floorboards of this version of the house hovering in space like the surreal victim of some semi-mythical tornado from the planes of mid-west America. Curious to find out, we began to scale down as quickly as possible. But a large golden eagle flew by and picked the dwarf off in its talons and took him away screaming, white feathers from his seagull cloak left floating around in confusion, beginning their slow see-saw journey towards the distant ground below. Suspended halfway between heaven and earth, Amy and I looked at each other and began to feel exposed and scared. *I think it's a dream! Try to wake up!* —I thought I heard her shouting to me over the howling of the wind, but it was hard to be certain. I thought to myself it also sounded a bit like *I drink ice cream, I'm tired of your make-up . . .*

I regained consciousness slumped across our dining table in the slanting yellow January sunlight, with Amy standing over me panicking, splashing cold water on my face. For some obscure reason it appeared that I had fainted at her first mention of a house near the station covered in ivy, and everything since had been part of a fevered hallucination or dream. Or so I thought. Then I heard the intense high-pitched chirping of birds again, this time followed by a loud cracking from the wall behind me. Amy and I stood up and turned around and backed away. The rear wall of our house had just split open, and the crack was widening from one moment to the next, plaster reigning down, as if a minor earthquake was in progress. Then we saw it: the crack opened further to reveal a grass-choked crevice with several birds' nests in it, each full of hungry little beaks filling the world with eager sounds of angry life and avian impatience. The white wall seemed to have become a chalk-white sea cliff, teaming with birds. As we approached it now with renewed curiosity, our fear replaced by wonder, the sunshine outside intensified and seemed to fill the room and our whole field of vision with golden light. The walls and cliffs gradually dissolved and moved aside, like a cracking egg revealing its yoke, like parting stage curtains, until we found ourselves walking barefoot, hand in hand, out across a vast sandy beach over which numerous seagulls were wheeling in high exhilarating arcs.

The tide was far out, but as we walked towards the distant sea I looked over my shoulder to see that a black horse and rider had just left the rocky shore and were galloping across the beach to meet us, throwing up sand, leaving fabulously dramatic footprints. *Where are we now?* —Amy asked me, pleasantly bewildered. *Your reality or mine or somebody else's?*

I don't know for sure, mine I think, I muttered, confused and strangely drowsy. The horse came closer and I saw that it was the dwarf again. He circled us once, then he bravely leapt off, leaving the wild stallion with its flowing black mane to gallop towards, and eventually vanish into, the distantly crashing waves. The dwarf wore boots and black baggy trousers and shirt, something vaguely Turkish. He drew a little sword from a scabbard on a belt around his waist, then knelt down and began drawing on the sand. Soon I recognised the diagrams: they were the same ones that I remembered Amy and I drawing at the table as she tried to explain the location of the non-existent house to me. Or had that only been a deranged dream or after dinner sleep?

I began to hear church bells, bells like the ones I so often hear on Sunday mornings. The dwarf seemed to notice how the sound caught my attention somewhat more than his drawings in the sand. He stood up, and with a theatrical flourish of his arms drew our gaze towards something which had previously eluded our notice. There was a great valley opening up in the sand about half a mile away, in which we could see the black shapes of the church spires and rooftops of a buried village. We began to walk towards it, while he, remaining silent all the time, ran and circled excitedly behind and around us like a happy dog. *Have you ever noticed that the dead are always silent, unable to speak when they reappear to us in dreams?* —Amy asked me dreamily. *A woman from Korea told me that once, and that's on the other side of the world, symptomatic of a universal principle perhaps . . .*

When we reached the valley in the sand we began to descend the path down towards the lost village, whose ancient and forgotten architectural features seemed to be coming more and more into clear detail as time went on. Then with a jolt of my senses, I realised that Amy and I were descending hand in hand into a mere reflection in a pool of water. Fortunately a breeze and a frond of seaweed had just drifted across the illusion, shattering the perfect mirror, and quite possibly saving our lives. It appeared too late for the dwarf, however, who we could not see or find, no matter how we looked about.

Gradually my vision and my whole perception shifted again, and I found myself back sitting at the dining room table on Sunday morning. The lake of still water in front of us had turned into a pool of olive oil which Amy had spilled on the smooth black polished surface of our table. For the next two minutes I watched in silent fascination as she slowly and methodically mopped every spot of it up with a cloth, in long circular swishing movements, left to right and back again, erasing all my momentary dreams and illusions, returning me to the safe and grounded, grindingly familiar world.

Then out of the corner of my eye I thought I saw something nudge up above the soil of the plant pot we keep sitting on the floor next to our patio doors. The pot holds a Meranta or *Prayer Plant*, which spookily folds all its leaves up at nightfall while making little noises which make you think for a moment there's someone else in the room with you. Now an ovoid form dripping with soil lifted up from among the roots of the plant, and a long octopus tentacle lashed out and wrapped around Amy's ankle.

Pausing, cloth in hand, just about to the leave the table, she looked at me, eyebrow raised, before beginning to slowly turn her head back to look towards the room's corner.

BIRD BRAINS

I

I used to be a particle physicist you know. No, really, I'm not shitting you. But of course these days I'm just a drunk. Most drunks drink to forget, but I drink to forget something that hasn't happened yet? Confused? You, as they say, will be. I'll just cut to the chase right now then, shall I? I'm not a tease. The Large Hadron Collider will soon create an event which has only happened once before in Earth's history. On that occasion, it was an accident caused by a meteor strike. Yes, the same one that wiped out the dinosaurs. But it didn't just wipe out them and other life forms, it reversed the polarity of the Earth's magnetic field and thereby reversed the arrow of time on this planet. Now, I know you'll be starting to struggle with the implications of that, so did I at first. *At first*, now what was it at first that put me on to this idea? —This idea that grew inside my head until it became an obsession and then as I progressively confirmed it with one test and experiment after another: a terrifying fact. Am I talking too fast for you?

Dinosaurs. This is so obvious that you're going to kick yourself when you hear it. They had feathers. Archaeologists and scientists have been progressively accepting this over the last twenty years as more fossils confirming it have come to light. Nobody seemed bothered by this except for me. But feathers make no sense on dinosaurs. They are hollow under a microscope, a highly evolved adaptation to combine incredible lightness with the ability to give uplift in flight. A large heavy flightless carnivore would have no need for them. *Unless*, unless. Unless time has reversed, and dinosaurs are going to evolve from the birds we have now, here in our present, and their feathers are just leftover traces from that. Why would they evolve like that? They would do it if there was a catastrophic event which wiped out all large mammals and left them as the dominant and ascendant species on earth. They would do that if that same event reversed the direction of time.

If you think this is crazy then I'll give you ten minutes to go away and look up time reversal on your beloved internet and then come back to me. It's accepted as completely possible at the level of particle physics, and only questionable at our macro level due to the inherently entropic nature of organic life. Entropy, energy constantly being lost, things decay and die, shit happens. A reverse-direction universe would be anti-entropic, energy would be being created all the time. Sounds rather joyous actually. Something for nothing, things appearing out of thin air. Gravity, interestingly, is a time-neutral event. Think about it. Toss a ball up in the air and it comes down to earth, or a ball fires itself off the ground and loops down into your hand which then lowers it back down to earth again. Perfect symmetry. Something organic, like baking a cake or gunning down thirty unarmed civilians, on the other hand, looks pretty different depending on time direction. Cake made from ingredients, people turned into worm food. Cake turned into flour, living people made out of soil. Quite a magic trick.

If only the damned birds didn't exist. I know we all love their songs and their pretty colours, me as much as the next guy, but their mere existence tells us that a time-reversal event is due soon in order to start turning them back into dinosaurs. If they weren't here then we could conclude that only one time-reversal event occurred in Earth's history and it's been going forward ever since, and was going backwards all the time before. You making sense of this? I'm thirsty, man. That old bag over there behind the counter doesn't serve me anymore. I've got money. You buy me a couple of bottles of whisky with this cash and I'll come back and tell you some more of this next week, give you time to get your head around it. We got ourselves a deal?

You looked me up, really? Wow, I'm impressed and flattered. You believe me now, I really did work at CERN. I was drummed out for alcohol problems? Well, they would say that, wouldn't they? To discredit me, of course, as a scientific heretic. They're worse than the Spanish Inquisition these days, the scientific community. Cruelly intolerant of all forms of dissent. Take it from me, man, I got their sharp end right up my jacksy. You want more proof of my theories? Another couple of bottles first please. I might even show you my laboratory, if you're nice to me.

Bit of a mess this place, sorry. My wife Marie left me six months ago. Understandable really, I don't blame her. It was all the dead birds that got to her I think, and the glass chambers and the electrical wires. You want a drink, my friend? Really? You sure? I think you're going to need one when you see this shit. Here, mind your feet there, just step over the transformer and compressor . . . that's liquid nitrogen that tube, don't want to freak you, but be careful, you bust that one and you'll know all about it. Right, follow me, just up a couple of ladders now into the attic. You're not claustrophobic or anything are you? Good. No terror of birds either? Terror of birds in confined spaces? Good, you're cut out for this job. You sure you're not a reporter, mister? You do seem ideal for this.

I know, I know. Now you know where I've been putting all the empty bottles. Nothing goes to waste in this household. Nor in this garden. The suburbs still supply a fine selection of bird species, despite mankind's ravages of the erstwhile biological diversity of the Belgian countryside through pollution and over-development. Yeah, just shift those notebooks out the way, make yourself a seat there, get comfortable. You sure you don't want a drink? This will take a while at first until the equipment heats up, until your eyes adjust to the hazy atmosphere. Chemicals, drugs? No man, a bit of formaldehyde here and there, a few free radicals and ionised trace elements, argon and helium, nothing harmful.

I'm glad you took a drink in the end. I knew you'd change your attitude. I can see I've gone and blown your mind, you poor bastard. Here, would you like me to let one out to play on your lap? He won't bite too hard, their teeth are still quite delicate when they're first coming in. Ha ha! Look at the little critter go! I'll set a few more out and we can see them play with each other. Little monsters, make human children look well behaved, I can tell you. This little guy here, the orange one, I call him Hubert, I made him out of a chaffinch who I reversed half a million times, took me three years. Three years of setting the chamber going, stopping, starting again, making him into an egg then watching his parents appear then ringing the neck of the male and setting the female going again. Poor old men, we really are history's janitors, the dogsbodies, while women do all the important work in evolutionary terms.

Could I do that to a human? What a sick frigging idea, mate. I'd need a lot bigger glass chambers for a kick-off, which would be higher technology than I can lay my hands on here in suburban Antwerp. And Christ, watching two real live adult human beings appear out of nothing then knowing you have to kill one of them? That would be a real horror movie. You want another drink? Hell, this is just me playing around with some poor rodents, sky rats. You'll forgive me if

I don't display quite the sentimentality for the little flying feckers that my fellow men and women do, but maybe that's because I know they're going to take over the planet. The meek shall inherit the Earth it says in the bible, and it's rarely wrong, about that or anything else. The birds are going to inherit the sky, actually, then everything.

Hello again. Good to see you, mate. You don't look so good, I tell you. Grey about the eyes, a tad unshaven, if I might say so. Not that I'm entitled by any means to regard myself as a paragon of good health and sartorial elegance, but hey I'm just a wino, remember, not married with a good job and stuff? Really? Man, I'm sorry to hear that, you sound like you could do with a friend to talk to, a good drink. Say, you got some money on you? Let's treat ourselves to a couple of crates each and make a weekend of it, what do you say?

Well, now you've nearly seen it all, eh, Adam? I know that's not your real name, but I'm going to rename you, the first man you see, the first man other than me of course, to set eyes upon this stuff. I don't count because I'm not a man anymore. I'm a god, because I can create life and destroy it, because I've seen the true hidden meaning of life, understood it and mastered it and put it to use. Maybe that's all gods are, people who've found out the real way of things and learned to rise above it all. That blackbird and those two starlings are coming on nicely, aren't they? We might let them out later. Things get really interesting when the booze runs out and you start to sober up on the third day. You've not been through that stage, so this will be your first time. Usually in the middle of the night, I find I'll wake up and all the wee critters will be oozing out of the plasterboard ceiling and the sarking boards, running all over your skin and pecking at you. It makes you panic at first, the first couple of times, then I learned to just laugh about it. Wave after wave of avian invasion washing over you, a little foretaste of all that's to come for the rest of humanity.

I picked up a copy of *Le Monde* from a waste paper basket the other day and saw that those raving lunatics at CERN are going ahead with that experiment soon, the one I warned them about. The end is nigh, my friend, want another drink of this bottle? —Still a little left, before we have to settle in for the thaw-out and the shakes. Delirium Tremens is the correct Latin medical term for the effect, I believe. Hallucinations. Cold Turkey is the druggie's version. Cold chicken for us maybe, eh? Get it? Squawk squawk, flap flap. It gets better every time. Last weekend the west gable dissolved, just slid away like a magic carpet and their leader, the bird god Loplop fluttered in to visit me. The surrealist artist Max Ernst used to do collages about him. About four feet high, red plumage and nasty looking talons but wearing a gentleman's waistcoat and top hat and talking in a kind of metallic croaking tone of voice like a crow. He sang me a song that changed all the colours in the sky, which turned my fingers in to the fine green fronds of a primordial palm waving in a swamp breeze. I got real hot and my mouth filled with sand, sweating tropical rivers. Man, I was suddenly so dried up and gagging, I got up and followed him out and tripped then flew across the suburban rooftops, flew down a few chimneys together until we found ourselves outside the local supermarket. The local MP was doing the rounds in his black suit, shaking hands and kissing babies in the lead-up to the next elections. But me and Loplop rumbled him, we saw the feathers sticking out of his shirt, the beak concealed under his four-o'-clock shadow.

We liberated the headless frozen chickens in the meat counter and led them all a merry dance like the pied piper, up and down the aisles and out into the street where they terrified the old ladies. How we laughed. The birds are coming back to life. Even your eggs and your omelettes aren't safe. You've been murdering birds for years, centuries, millennia. But they won't stand for it much longer. If you can't beat them, join them. Beat them, eggbeater, get it? I'm with the birds, and we're coming to get you. Drink eases the pain of knowing I'm a traitor, and it helps me to fly, fly like they do, and to see it all from above from where everything looks so small, so arbitrary, so fragile. You all think you're in charge, but you're nothing, an accident of history because the tide went your way for a while. But what does tide do? It goes out again, and reveals all the flapping fish suffocating, the washed up crabs and stones and fossils. And then it washes all your footprints away until there's nothing. Nothing but a few cryptic clues that everybody misses. Look at me. Like I said, I used to be a particle physicist, but now I'm just a drunk.

II

Monsieur Oiseau is just the nickname the children of La Chapelle call him. Rumour has it he is actually a form of bipedal dinosaur, approximately man-height, the result of some grotesque experiment undertaken by the missing and discredited mad Belgian scientist Henri Vermeulen, who lost his job under mysterious circumstances at CERN in 2012. No authenticated photographs have yet emerged of Oiseau, despite numerous supposed sightings and ongoing investigations by Swiss, Belgian, and French undercover police agencies. Paris is a big place. Sightings have also been reported in the 18th arrondissement. Monsieur Oiseau seems to only emerge at night in poorly lit areas, usually in overcast conditions when even moonlight is limited. He wears a long dark grey raincoat and hat and strangely shaped boots which have been adapted to hold his talons, some of which have been seen to protrude through the leather in places. Oiseau's movements appear odd, even at a distance, resembling human walking only superficially. His progress is generally slow and furtive, but on occasions when he has been challenged by ill-intentioned adolescents he has been seen to move off at a phenomenal speed, sometimes removing his ungainly footwear in order to do so. A video on YouTube, unauthenticated and possibly a fake, purports to show a shady figure sprinting down Rue d'Orsel at a speed in excess of seventy miles an hour, far in excess of human capability. This might provide a clue as to why the creature has so far proven so elusive and evaded capture. A spate of stray dog carcasses found in 2013 was connected for a while with the Oiseau rumours, as was an unusual number of disappearances of homeless men and drug-addicts last winter, followed by accusations that the Gendarmerie had been implicated in a cover-up in order to reduce the risk of panic among the wider Parisian population. The impression that Oiseau seems to limit his appearances to the poorer immigrant areas of the capital has fuelled social discontent and the suspicion that not enough has been done to address the danger. Some sceptics maintain that this bird-man is an urban myth, a projection of social division and simmering racial tensions in a city where far-right politics and large ethnic populations sit uncomfortably side by side.

III

The shouting children and ragged street people scare her. Her creator, or her father (as she thinks of him) Professor Vermeulen named her Sappho, and this is the name she thinks of herself with. She only wants to be left alone, but paradoxically; the dense chaotic streets of a major European city are actually the safest hiding place she has been able to devise. She needs a ready food source, and the poor and the homeless seem to her to have been discarded by the wider populace, pushed aside like the unfinished dirty dinner plates of overfed aristocrats. Vermeulen showed her films of human history. She understands a great deal of it, in so far as any rational being can, or at least all she needs to. Her large green eyes, slit as vertically and merciless as a hawk's are generally enough to paralyse any would-be assailant at close quarters, through sheer shock. Her powerful prehensile tale is also extremely useful and unexpected in any contretemps with mammalian bipeds.

Of course she is a female. This is how it works, the Matryoshka Doll principle as Vermeulen explained it. She is the product of a localised time-reversal experiment, and so her metabolism and development are anti-entropic. She is getting slowly younger in other words, and in several years' time will finally have to seek out a safe and secluded hideaway in which to regress to the size of a helpless chick and synthesise finally into a beautiful turquoise egg the size of a basketball. Then the most mysterious and miraculous thing of all will happen: both her adult parents will spontaneously emerge out of the ether as the egg deliquesces into its component parts. Without the professor on hand for the first time, of course, nobody will be able to supervise the destruction of the unnecessary male, and so the danger will emerge of the population starting to grow and expand over time from that point forward. Starting out as fully grown intelligent adults, will present this new reptilian race with a distinct evolutionary advantage over its human counterparts. If they can stay undetected and breed and expand in covert locations dispersed across Europe, then in time they may present a real threat to the current human dominance of the planet.

For now Sappho enjoys her evening walk by the Seine, walks down the narrow streets of the Île Saint-

Louis wrapped in the perceptual scarf of winter fog, and gazes in the windows of the antique shops. On the next corner she spies a fine ladies hat with peacock feathers in it, and on a whim her claw smashes the glass and she struts in to seize it. Two blocks on, a police car pulls up at a crossroads, blocking a street end, and she regrets having been so foolhardy to have ventured this near for the first time to the city centre and the middle-class areas. The two uniformed guards getting out either side of the vehicle ahead look better fed than her usual choice of dinner partner. She surmises that they are probably more likely to be missed too, stitched in to the whole wider fabric of human society, social pack animals that they are. Foregoing the chance to taste their flesh, she instead simply scrambles vertically straight up the four-storey façade of the Haussmann tenement immediately to her right and scuttles and flutters away across the rooftops.

Later she makes her way to one of the towers of the west façade of Notre Dame, a nice flat lead roof in which she can feast on a Korean tourist with a side salad of Algerian pick-pocket, both plucked from the richly-stocked streets below. Her short vestigial feathers are quite adequate to keep her warm, even at this altitude in the chill easterly breeze of oncoming winter, and her wings, though short and ineffectual, will certainly suffice to help her glide back down in due course, should a rapid descent be necessary to evade capture before daybreak.

The way home does not prove as inconsequential as she has hoped. Driven down into the underground to escape the pursuit of three police cars with irritating flashing lights and wailing sirens, she takes a wrong turning, failing to find the sewer entrance where she thought she remembered one, arriving instead at a busy train platform packed with opera-goers in furs and shawls, preparing to head home to their elegant well-to-do suburbs. She is their worst nightmare, the ultimate immigrant, a refugee not just from another country but from another time. The humans don't realise it, but one of their most unwittingly effective weapons against her is their screaming when they are panicked, since it causes intense pain and disturbance to her vastly superior hearing system, evolved to let her detect herds of prey moving up to twenty-five miles away across the great plains of central Asia.

Forced onto an underground train in confusion, she bounds through all six carriages at speed leaving dazzled and petrified passengers in her wake before smashing her way out the front cabin and into the darkness of the tunnel beyond, swiftly taking the drivers yelling head off as much to silence him as by way of a snack. She finds an entrance from the Metro tunnels to the sewer system at last, which she usually knows and remembers well, but after a few miles this new section blocks her way unexpectedly so that, knowing daybreak is dangerously near, she has to take the ultimate last resort and rise up through a street gully on Rue Saint-Denis. A gypsy beggar, playing an accordion cross-legged on the pavement next to her point of emergence, looks up at her in awe as his polka grinds down to a sagging halt in his disbelieving arms. Too full to eat any more, but resourceful enough never to give up, she holds her talons out towards him and lets her long tongue salivate over his face until he parts with his coat and hat and instrument as invited and runs off gibbering.

The streets are not yet busy enough for anyone to have witnessed the truth before she completes her new disguise and kneels down over the accordion and begins to puzzle over how to coax passable human music from the instrument. The sun is up now, so this seems as reasonable a strategy as any for a place to hide until the next nightfall. Wrapped up under old blankets, doubtless passers-by will just mistake her for the tragic victim of some disfiguring disease. In this shady corner by a train station, who will attempt to look past the overhanging brim of her hat or the folds of her tattered old coat? Whoever wants to meet the eyes of a beggar anyway? But if they do they will doubtless be rendered magically speechless and unable thereafter to be believed.

IV

For the benefit of the tape, this interview is between Henri Vermeulen and Officers Bertrand and DeBeer of Interpol. A consultant scientist and psychologist, Professor Mousavi and Doctor Brezinka, are also in attendance.

Q: *We thought you were dead, Monsieur Vermeulen. Where have you been hiding and why have you decided to re-emerge in plain sight after so long?*

A: *It's Professor Vermeulen to you, actually. Brussels is a big place. I began to realise I was missing a relative of mine in Paris so I decided to come through and visit her here at* last. You may have heard of her: six feet tall with feathers and a beak and talons.

Q: *Your inappropriately joking reference is, we presume to the so-called Monsieur Oiseau phenomenon. Can you tell us please of the whereabouts of this creature and its true nature?*

A: *As her only guardian in the world I had a moral duty to protector her from you people for as long as possible. Her name was Sappho by the way, she was female and she was as intelligent as you are, possible more so in your particular case.*

Q: *We notice you are talking of her in the past tense, Monsieur Vermeulen.*

A: *Quite so. She finally deliquesced into an egg a month ago after a six month period of vulnerable childhood during which period I watched over and cared for her. She has now been replaced by her two adult parents. Ha. I see that got your attention. No, I won't be telling you their whereabouts any time soon. Then again, I don't need to. Have any of you got the exact time on you?*

Q: *We're asking the questions, but it's about five minutes to noon. Why?*

A: *Then I suggest you get your televisions and internet fired up and get ready for a very interesting news story which will be breaking.*

Q: *We are on guard for your notorious pranks and halluci-*
nations, Monsieur Vermeulen. Your file describes in detail
your sorry record as a hopeless alcoholic and social misfit.

A: *Oh, but I thawed out years ago. Woke up and smelt the*
coffee, as those damned Americans say with their invasion
of Franglais. I kicked the bottle the day my little dino-birds
started getting sentient and calling me daddy. Father-
hood brings out the best in even the worst of us, wouldn't
you say? I'll take that as a yes. Since you seem intent in
persisting in acting like complete dullards with your line
of questioning, perhaps I should just start imparting the
relevant and required scientific information, shall I? Your
two so-called experts sitting there may at least understand
some of it, even if you don't.

Q: *Mister Vermeulen. Henri . . .*

A: *Ever heard of T-symmetry? The theoretical reversal of*
the vector of time at the quantum level? Good. One of you
at least. I've tried warning CERN about this and they won't
listen so this is why I have been driven to this, this campaign
of avian terror, if you want to think of it that way. Accord-
ing to my estimates and calculations and the latest scientific
papers I've been able to get my hands on: CERN will under-
take the T-symmetry experiment sometime around summer
2020. We don't have much time left therefore, quite literally.
We have to stop them from doing that. It will set a series
of events in motion that will reverse the direction of time
and humanity will begin moving backwards, de-evolving,
generation by generation. Nobody will even be aware of this
of course, because they will be trapped within their own
biological framework from which everything will appear

indistinguishable from normal. The net effect, however, will be that this planet's future will have been aborted, we will be heading back towards the dinosaur age when creatures like my friends Castor and Pollux ruled the earth, and were probably doing rather a good job of it before a meteor struck the Yucatan peninsula.

Q: *You're losing all of us, Professor. Castor and Pollux?*

A: *Sappho's parents. Have you any idea how rare fossils are? To become one, you have to be very stupid and lie down to wait to die on a river bed. Ninety-nine percent of the species that have been and gone upon this world would never have been so daft or so unfortunate. I know, too mind-blowing to think about, isn't it? —Which may be why most people don't. We therefore know almost nothing of the vast arrays of species, including intelligent dinosaurs, and intelligent forbears of modern birds, that once lived on Earth. Sappho's parents are examples of such. She and I prepared films and books to teach them about our world when they arrived and to treat me as their parent, the one human being they could trust, the exception that proves the rule. I saddled up Castor last night and flew here on his back, an exhilarating nocturnal journey across the rooftops of Paris, I can tell you. Sappho used to pluck her feathers so that she could conceal herself in human clothes, but her parents are not going to be so shy. We've decided to start a sort of public information campaign, and my turning myself in was just the start of it. When people see the evidence splashed across their screens, they're finally going to start believing all the crank stories I've been leaking onto the internet for the last ten years. I'm not the mad scientist, CERN are, and they need to be stopped. Like I say, turn on your television. By now I estimate that the French President should be as besieged as a pile of pumpkin seed in his offices by a giant bird pecking all the glass out of his windows, and the custodians of a certain famous tourist landmark should be starting to regret all those vindictive anti-pigeon measures . . .*

V

The Eiffel Tower was only supposed to be a temporary building. The thought is always buried in the back of the mind of every visitor, Parisian and foreigner alike. Those lifts bounce to a worrying degree as they stop at each floor. Today the effect is heightened by the unexpected arrival of a two metre high bird with vibrant red and orange plumage, savage green eyes and vicious beak alighting on the top of the lift car and attempting to bite its way through the cables. For weeks, nervous local jokes have been used to mask the Parisians' growing disquiet at proliferating rumours of the wing beats of huge birds being heard flapping over the rooftops on dark nights, and of disturbingly loud thumps heard on flat roofs overhead, as if something monstrous is strutting about up there.

Bored with the lift carriages, whose emergency brakes prevent catastrophic descent even after the cables are severed in any case, Pollux makes her way up to the viewing platform itself, which the proud city fathers so wisely enclosed in a decorative cage to prevent suicides many decades beforehand. The mesh is mostly dense enough to prevent her beak penetrating too far, although a few appendages are lost proving the issue, not to mention several strokes and heart attacks. The point, as ever in our brave new media-savvy world, is publicity. The footage of sixty terrified men women and children being pecked at and hounded and tormented by a giant bird with vicious talons and a particularly blood-curdling screech, three hundred and twenty metres above Pairs, will certainly burn its way indelibly into the public retina. Pollux is also actually quite a gentle and intellectual creature at other times, but has been told to play up stereotypical expectations for the cameras. As a cynical man once said, nobody ever lost a fortune underestimating the public intelligence. She will fly off before the army helicopters and fighter jets get here, or maybe bring a few down on the way for her amusement. The tourists will be mostly rescued and unharmed, led away in single file down the seldom-used escape stairs. But the point will have been made. In the complacent minds of all the self-satisfied bourgeois French and in the soiled underpants of their president. Shout the news from the rooftops. History is attacking us, fuelled by our blind ignorance of it, on which it feeds. The threat is here, it is upon us. Not from foreign immigrants and terrorists but from ourselves. Not from elsewhere, but elsewhen.

GALLOWAY OCTUPLETS

1
Corsewall Woods

Summer morning remembering
scintillation of boyhood holidays
the light of dawn fresh
and rich as local milk
glimpsed through fronds
of old tall trees, cool
from the whispering leaf shade
into unreachable brightness
across ripening fields
a white house distant
whose green hill conceals
the sea beyond, imagined
sparkling.

2
Loch Ryan

As the long waves roar
caress the endless strand
turn over shingle
sifted fine as sand
the age-old thoughts
now pace the boundary
that narrows out
where land and sea merge
in milky watercolour
for the first time finding
sized to fill my fist
an undamaged oyster shell
each to its aeon between tides
one life in the balance
empty, open, all pearls gone
silk mouth spilling only dust
a perfectly phrased question
to close the heart around.

3
Treetops

In the flat above the stables
thrust up into the sky
as babes in the woods
the trees rustle about us
sleeping minds brim full
of dream and nightmare
a thousand straining bodies
the souls of labourers
who worked on this estate
tethered to the ground
by trunk and roots
of blustering leaves
an earthbound ocean.

4
Dunskey

The old sluice gate wheel
rusted, no longer turns
from the cool lily pond
no water escapes
the stream run dry
beside the darkened pathway
strewn with purple petals
fallen from the tangled bowers
arching over, a green tunnel
from light into shade.

5
Sleep

Year on year the weight
of sleep accumulates
each morning struggling
further up from glaucous depths
one day the iron of those chains
my sluggish arms will baulk
then eyes and mouth opening
find that they can *breathe-see*
the vast dark intersecting
maze of dreams of all life gone
and yet to be, a kingdom
of torpor labyrinthine,
sovereign of half the earth
dreamer of the other.

6
Daybreak

Omni-directional energy
a breaking wave of life
nursing itself
from darkness into light
at the stable doors
a little girl unleashes
a flurry of spaniel puppies
squealing scrambling
over each other
to be lifted up
in her mothering arms
everyone new to their roles
yet supremely gifted.

7
Castle Kennedy

Captured and contained
nearly tame, Nature flourishes
within the walled garden
where all paths curve back
pointing towards
the ever-timely lesson
those castle ruins devoured
by ivy and wisteria.
Although our violation
of her always reeks
Nature manages
even erasing us
beauty.

8
Port Logan

The slow curving bay
draws up above its sandline
the queer crop of millennia of grinding
bricks turned to smooth orange pebbles
concrete from sea walls, chains and posts
iron of anchors become red balls of rust
granite, gabbro, quartz, sandstone
all intermixed in metamorphic
volcanic marbles fit to awe a child
spheres striated exotically
as alien worlds, fragments of bright glass,
pottery forgetting the hands that once
shaped and coveted them
become cryptic, fleeting jewels
hefty timber posts from piers
in the end are lightweight lozenges,
skittish as balsa all become sand
here finally none withstand
except what we made ourselves
towards the close, to paraphrase Larkin:

what will survive of us is not love
but plastic: in all senses
how we've learned to mess with molecules
love, we think our grand human contrivance
perhaps only cerebral accretion around
animal instinct core mere glue
of valency, attempted pair bonding
none the less magisterial and mysterious
how it can endlessly change state
but persist like memory, durable, indigestible,
obstinate, altered but never destroyed
we pollute the universe with Eros
with our damned seed, endless explosion
of pure pain of self-knowledge
we who shiver before mirrors
as well we might. Stand here
at the world's edge waiting
for the wind to drop.

ACKNOWLEDGEDMENTS

Thanks to Rachel Kendall, who first publisher "Bright November" in her magazine *Sein Und Werden*. Thanks to Andrew Hook and Adam Lowe of Dog Horn who first published "Out Of The Box" in the anthology *punkPunk!* Thanks to Peter and Alison Buck of Elsewhen Press who first published "Bird Brains" in their anthology *Existence Is Elsewhen*. Thanks to Sally Evans who first published part 10 of "The Twelve Seasons" in *Poetry Scotland Magazine* (and to Carolyn Richardson who sent it to her) and again to Sally for later publishing "Galloway Octuplets" in the same magazine. Thanks to the editors at Snuggly Books for commissioning this unusual collection. Thanks to numerous other encouragers and friends from across the years too numerous to mention without risk of inadvertent favouritism.

Last but not least love and thanks in eternity to my brother Ally Thompson (1955-2016) for a lifetime's inspiration and the oil painting which we have used for the cover of this book. The website of Ally Thompson is at: www.glasgowsurrealist.com

A PARTIAL LIST OF SNUGGLY BOOKS

Lightning Source UK Ltd.
Milton Keynes UK
UKHW011112151219
355424UK00006B/208/P